KIDS CAN'T STOP READING
THE CHOOSE YOUR
OWN ADVENTURE® STORIES!

"Choose Your Own Adventure is the best thing that has come along since books themselves."
—Alysha Beyer, age 11

"I didn't read much before, but now I read my Choose Your Own Adventure books almost every night."
—Chris Brogan, age 13

"I love the control I have over what happens next."
—Kosta Efstathiou, age 17

"Choose Your Own Adventure books are so much fun to read and collect—I want them all!"
—Brendan Davin, age 11

And teachers like this series, too:

"We have read and reread, worn thin, loved, loaned, bought for others, and donated to school libraries our Choose Your Own Adventure books."

CHOOSE YOUR OWN ADVENTURE®—
AND MAKE READING MORE FUN!

THE UNDERGROUND RAILROAD

BY DOUG WILHELM

ILLUSTRATED BY RON WING

An R. A. Montgomery Book

BANTAM BOOKS
NEW YORK • TORONTO • LONDON • SYDNEY • AUCKLAND

RL 4, age 10 and up

THE UNDERGROUND RAILROAD
A Bantam Book / September 1996

CHOOSE YOUR OWN ADVENTURE® is a registered
trademark of Bantam Books,
a division of Bantam Doubleday Dell Publishing Group, Inc.
Registered in U.S. Patent and Trademark Office and elsewhere.

Original conception of Edward Packard

*Cover art by Gary Ciccarelli
Interior illustrations by Ron Wing*

ISBN 0-553-56744-6

Published simultaneously in the United States and Canada

Bantam Books are published by Bantam Books, a division of
Bantam Doubleday Dell Publishing Group, Inc. Its trademark,
consisting of the words "Bantam Books" and the portrayal of a
rooster, is Registered in U.S. Patent and Trademark Office and
in other countries. Marca Registrada. Bantam Books, 1540
Broadway, New York, New York 10036.

PRINTED IN THE UNITED STATES OF AMERICA
OPM   0 9 8 7 6 5 4 3 2 1

This book is dedicated to all the unsung heroes—black and white alike—of the Underground Railroad.

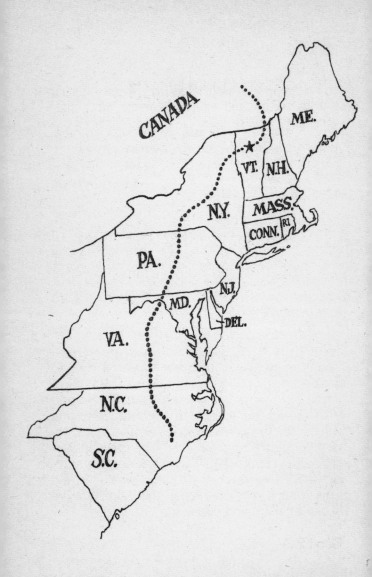

WARNING!!!

Do not read this book straight through from beginning to end. These pages contain many different adventures you may have when the Underground Railroad takes a detour through your northern Vermont town.

From time to time as you read along, you'll be asked to make a choice. What happens to you and those around you will be determined by what you choose. After you make your decision, follow the instructions to find out what happens to you next.

Some fugitive slaves from the South are trapped in a building near your home. You will have to decide what you are prepared to do to help them. But be careful! You won't know whom to trust. Your town is divided about slavery, and who knows—your next-door neighbor could report you to the slave hunters! The slave hunters are ruthless men. They will stop at nothing to recapture those slaves—no matter who is in the way. Your choice may mean the difference between freedom and disaster.

Good luck!

AUTHOR'S NOTE

Between its origins in the late 1700s and its end in the Civil War, the Underground Railroad helped uncounted thousands of black American slaves make their way to freedom. We don't really know how many, because records were rarely kept. The Underground Railroad wasn't actually a railroad—it was a multitude of secret routes by which free people, both white and black, helped slaves reach places where they too could be free. People who hid and fed fugitives along the way were called stationmasters; people who smuggled them to the next "station" were called conductors. Most of the traveling was done at night. Nearly all was done in secret, often with professional "slave hunters" in pursuit.

Until 1850, reaching freedom simply meant crossing the Mason-Dixon Line, which separated the Southern slave states from the free states in the North. Most Northern states allowed escaped slaves to settle there as free people. The notorious Fugitive Slave Act of 1850 changed all this.

According to the new law, anyone helping a runaway slave anywhere in the United States could be thrown into prison—and law officers in the North were required to help slave hunters capture the slaves and bring them back to the South. Many people were outraged by this law, and thousands defied it. Traffic on the Underground Railroad swelled in these last years before the Civil War. But now the escaping slaves had to be smuggled all the way to Canada.

One Northern state whose people were angriest about the Fugitive Slave Act was Vermont. Many Vermonters felt strongly about individual liberty, and they helped the fugitives however they could. Others, however, felt just as strongly that slaveholding was the Southerners' business, and that Northern abolitionists—those who felt slavery must be abolished—had no right to interfere. This split in opinion was often very emotional and sometimes even resulted in violence.

The Township of Randolph, in the hills of central Vermont, was a station on the Underground Railroad along one of its most important lines. Randolph is where I live today, and it's where I wrote this book. The places in the story are real: the village up on the ridge, which I call the Center, is known as Randolph Center today, and the town down in the valley really was called Slab City in 1853. Today it's just called Randolph. Three of the people in this story are real: the stationmaster Loren Griswold, his grandmother, the Indian healer Margery, and Joseph Poland, editor of the *Voice of Freedom* newspaper in Montpelier. The other people are made up—but they could have been real, just as the story you're about to step into could really have happened, in the heyday of the Underground Railroad.

Doug Wilhelm
Randolph, Vermont

They call this place Slab City. Not because it's a city—before the railroad came four years ago, it wasn't even much of a village. Up at the Center, in the posh houses along the ridgetop avenue, the quality folks look down on Slab City. Even the circus never used to come here.

But that was before the trains came.

"The railroad's changing everything," the sawmill workers say. "Slab City's on the map."

Everyone calls your town Slab City because the line of little sawmills down along the river always has piles of rough-sawn slabs of lumber outside. The mills are long, unpainted sheds, with dark openings at each end and the round, deadly saw glinting inside. The little river is lined with the waterwheels that turn the saws in the long sheds.

Turn to page 2.

Above the mills is a tavern for travelers. A covered bridge leads across the river toward a few scattered farms. But there wasn't much else over there until the railroad came. Now there's a sprawl of wooden stores, businesses, houses, even the school where you go. Except it's summer now, so you don't have to.

A short walk up the new Main Street is the railroad crossing. When the train churns through, it makes the whole town shudder, and it heaves up smoke that hovers in a long, dirty trail. You always know when the train's been by.

But there's another train. This one you can't see or hear. It's been running for decades. It's about to make a detour into Slab City. And when it does, it'll tear your new, proud, hard-working town in half.

The year is 1853, seven years before the Civil War.

Go on to the next page.

4

On a bright summer morning you're up the river above the village with your friend Zebediah. You're fishing with whittled saplings at a spot where smooth rocks slope into a bend in deep, clear water. You and Zeb have caught two big brook trout apiece. Now you dive alone into the chilly water.

You come up sputtering and joyful.

"Come on, Zeb!" you call to the boy perched on the slanted rocks. "You've done your work—caught your family a lunch. Even a Quaker ought to cool off."

Zeb's brow wrinkles as he looks up and down the river. He wears a coarse, dark shirt and heavy, dark trousers. The Quaker's wide-brimmed hat sits heavily on his head. But his face is freckled, and his eyes are twinkling.

"'Tisn't strictly permitted," Zeb says.

"'Tain't nobody watching," you answer, treading in the deep water.

Zeb checks again for onlookers.

"Thee won't tell?" he asks you.

"Have I ever?"

He nods, quickly strips off his clothes, and knifes in beside you.

Zeb's family are Friends—or Quakers. They live by a strict code of commandments. Your family is Congregationalist, and your fathers couldn't be more different. But the two of you have always stuck together. You've shared many secrets. But so far each secret, like this one, has been small. That's about to change forever.

Go on to the next page.

You splash, dive, and laugh until the summer sun is almost straight above you in the sky. Then you lie on the rocks until you're dry. You both draw on your clothes, and Zeb's freckles wrinkle as he pulls the stiff hat down on his forehead. You follow the river back to town.

The high Vermont hills rise above Slab City, both behind you and up ahead. The road climbs steadily toward the Center, three miles ahead up on the high ridge. Both the Center and Slab City are part of the Township of Randolph.

But you turn left at the tavern, cross the covered bridge, and head into the sprawl of new buildings. On a narrow street of small wooden homes, you see your mother waiting for you.

Something's wrong. Her face has been heavy with strain these recent weeks, but there's something more there now. Her eyes brighten when she sees your fish, and she smiles. But you're not fooled. You want to know what's going on.

Your mother takes the fish from your hand. Her fingers are dark with printer's ink.

"These'll please your pa," she says.

"Doubt that," you mutter.

"Please—be careful," she whispers, catching your arm. "He's feeling it badly today."

You nod and follow her into the kitchen.

"Ma," you say, as she puts the black skillet on the stove. "What is it? What's wrong?"

Your mother's shoulders tighten. She hesitates, then turns around.

"Something terrible has happened," she says.

Turn to page 76.

You peer out from behind the tree. As they come closer, you can see the pale-suited man. The other rider is the sheriff. Something seems missing.

As they come opposite you, the pale-suited rider holds out his arm. The two men stop, and the Southern gentleman gets down to look at pieces of hay on the road.

You draw back, knowing now what's wrong. You pull at the girl's sleeve, because you've got to run—run up into the dark woods, and fast. But before you can move, you hear a click behind you.

Turn to page 104.

8

You decide you have to try to help the runaways, if you can.

The rocks between the railroad ties punch at the callused bottoms of your feet. You find Dickey beyond them. He's sitting hunched over his arm.

"I want to go after them," you say. "Are you okay?"

"Yeah," he says, breathing hard. "I think so."

"I'll be back," you say.

"But . . ."

You don't stay to listen. You step cautiously into the cornfield, listening closely. The long leaves brush your face as you push the stalks aside. The moon has risen now, and the stalks all around you are pale in the moonlight. But you can't see more than a few feet ahead, and all you *can* see is more pale stalks.

You stop moving. Got to listen.

Except for vague rustling when the soft breeze filters through, the whole cornfield is silent. The hunter must be stopped and listening, the same as you. The same as the woman and her boy.

Turn to page 94.

Your friend pulls on your sleeve. The two of you retreat.

"Zeb," you whisper back in the dark mud-room, "why were we allowed in there? Why did I hear that?"

"Because we need help," Zeb whispers back. "I told my parents we can trust thee. I told them that even though thee is not a Friend, thee sees a light."

"What?"

"I mean that thee sees the right thing, and *usually* does it."

You can't help grinning. "Usually!"

But Zeb doesn't smile back. "This is one of those times," he says, looking into your eyes, "to do what is right."

Your grin fades. You nod.

"My parents are townsfolk," Zeb says. "We have no horse or carriage. We need new con-ductors—someone to bring the cargo to Mont-pelier."

"When? Soon?"

"Not soon," he says. "Now. Tonight."

Turn to page 100.

"I'd like to ride for it—try to outrun them," you say to Nat.

"Well," the farmer says, "you'll have to . . ."

There's a shuffling noise right behind you.

You spin around. Hay is falling off the pile as a dark figure shinnies out from beneath it. Nat's eyes dart around to see if anyone is watching, but no one seems to be.

The figure stands up. It's a girl, maybe twelve years old, with hay in her hair and a man's trousers cut off at the knees. She draws in a long breath as she quivers with a coming sneeze.

"*Don't*," Nat whispers. He whips a rag out of his pocket and covers the girl's nose. From beneath it comes a muffled eruption.

"Whew!" the girl says, her whole face twitching. "Two more seconds under that pile and I'd a had the sneezing fit of two lifetimes! Wouldn'ta cared *who* was listening." She grins crookedly at the two of you. "Sorry about coming out. Seemed like it was safe."

"Well, all right, then," Nat says, his narrow face creased and worried. "Let's get you two goin'. Those slave hunters don't quit easy."

"They been after us all the way since we left Maryland," the girl says. "They never quit at *all.*"

She looks at you. "But I come this far," she says. "I got to make it."

Turn to page 69.

The millworkers have the muscle to do something—to bust the captives free. What could you do alone? You decide to let them know.

It's almost suppertime, and the riverbank is crowded with workers heading home. Arriving on a run, you spot tall, long-armed Henry Briggam. You skitter down the bank and grab his arm, drawing him away from the crowd.

Henry's forehead wrinkles as he peers down at you. "What's all this?" he says, chuckling as you tug him aside. The other men turn to look.

"What's the big secret, kid?"

You're panting, struggling for breath. "Those slaves—the ones they caught at Mister Griswold's . . ."

"Yeah?" Now Henry is bending to you, big hands on his knees. "What do you know?"

"They're here in town. The hunters have them hid. They're waiting for the train."

Henry's eyes catch fire. "Where are they?"

You blink at the sudden ferocity on the big man's face. "Th-the second house above the lumber shed, by the tracks," you stammer. "The one that's empty. They're in there."

"Are you sure?"

"Yes. They're upstairs."

Henry stands up and turns to the watching crowd of men.

"They've got those poor captured slaves in our town," he shouts. "They're in a house by the tracks. Let's go stand up for liberty!"

A powerful roar rises from the crowd.

Turn to page 84.

Dobbs gives Dickey some water. He carries the boy into his office and sets him on a couch.

The stationmaster draws out his heavy trainman's pocket watch.

"The train south to White River Junction is due in thirty minutes," he says. "If that man has recaptured those fugitives, he'll be coming in here with them quite soon."

He stands for a moment, thinking.

"All right," he says quickly. "Do you know where Devon Hawke, the blacksmith, lives?"

"Yes."

"How about Jacob Jackson, the Congregationalist minister? Thomas Lantman, the shoemaker? Arthur Newell, the grocer's assistant? Ronald Neely, the carpenter?"

At each name you nod.

"Then run to their homes as fast as you can," Dobbs says. "Tell them an urgent matter requires the society, and they must be on the depot platform at nine P.M. sharp. Not in the station—tell them to come to the platform outside. You've got twenty minutes. Get going! I'll see to the boy."

You don't understand what you're doing exactly, but you dash out the door. Slab City is small enough that you're able to knock on every man's door within minutes. Without pausing a heartbeat, each man nods at your news and runs out into the night.

It's almost nine as you trot back toward the depot, wondering what this "society" is.

Turn to page 106.

Below the tavern, in the shade of a sawmill, millworkers sit on a pile of slabs. Their undershirts are soaked with sweat. They're eating coarse bread and cheese and drinking cider for lunch.

You hover nearby, a familiar eavesdropper. Two of the strong, shaggy men, one tall and the other dark and stocky, stand face-to-face. Their fists are clenched as they glare into each other's eyes. A knot of millworkers stands behind the men.

"Blast it, Henry, it's a *property* matter," says the dark, stocky man. "People have a right to bring stolen property back."

"The hell they do," says Henry, the tall, rangy one. His tone is level but fierce. "Slaves ain't slabs of wood, Zachariah—they're human beings the same as you and me. Just 'cause a person's born in Maryland or Carolina don't mean they got any less right to walk around free than a Vermonter has."

"The law says slaves are property," Zachariah answers. "You saying freemen shouldn't follow the law?"

"That law is *wrong*!" the tall man thunders. "I'm saying if any slave hunters were ever fools enough to set foot in Slab City, this'd be as far as they'd get. I promise you that."

"You'd have to deal with more than the slave hunters, then, Henry," the dark man says. "You'd have to deal with us." He raises a threatening fist. Henry knocks it away.

"Hey, you men," someone shouts from within the nearest shed. "Back to work!"

Turn to page 80.

Zeb leads you through the mudroom, where boots are stacked on drying racks, and through the family's kitchen. You've been in these rooms before many times. But now Zeb leads you further, into the front part of the Bates home.

You follow your friend to the doorway of the family's parlor, where you've never been or dreamed of going. Here, in the doorway's shadow, you stop.

Before you in their solemn gray and white clothes stand Samuel and Rebeccah Bates, Zeb's mother and father. They nod hello, as if they too have been waiting for you.

But that's not the biggest surprise.

Beside Samuel stands Loren Griswold. Silver-haired and hatless, Mister Griswold is the last person in the world you expected to see. Of course he doesn't live in Slab City—his fine brick home is up in the Center. He is the township's most dignified citizen, a former Vermont state senator and the head of Randolph's oldest family. He would never normally pay a visit to an ordinary schoolteacher like Samuel Bates.

But Loren Griswold is also the "stationmaster" of your township's station on the Underground Railroad. At least, he was until yesterday.

"We have a serious situation to contend with," Mister Griswold is telling the Bates family.

I'll say we do, you think. Should you tell them the captives are in Slab City—and that you know where they are?

Turn to page 53.

"This is *not* the way," your mother hollers. She faces one group of men, then turns to confront the other. "You'll kill each other."

"Maybe that *is* the way," a big man growls. "Maybe there's no other."

Both bunches of men mutter agreement. They start to push toward each other. The women are crowded on both sides—they're standing firm, but you're scared. Suddenly there's a shout behind you.

"Hey, you men—all of you!"

The men turn. You whirl around.

It's your father.

Beside him stands a man in a dark business suit. Beside *him* is the sheriff.

Your father raises his loud mill sawyer's voice as he waves at the dark-suited man.

"Men," he says, "this is a matter of law. The man beside me is the circuit judge for this part of Vermont. He happened to be at the Mansion House Tavern this afternoon, on account of a legal matter that concerns the two people being held in this house."

The crowd quiets down to hear.

Go on to the next page.

The judge steps forward. "Vermont law says any fugitive slave captured in this state will be taken under the protection of the nearest circuit judge," he announces. "That is what I intend to do. I can assure you that all the rights that pertain to this matter—including the right of property—will be considered in my decision."

The judge starts for the door of the house. But the antislavers bar his way.

"What about *human* rights?" one of them demands.

The judge faces the antislavers. They're not moving.

Turn to page 95.

"Now listen, both of you," Nat says. "See those big trees up that little rise?"

He points toward a grove of thick-trunked trees set in even ranks on a gentle slope.

"That sugarbush belongs to a man down to the village," Nat says.

The girl leans toward you. "What's a sugarbush?" she whispers.

You blink in surprise. "Why, it's maple trees— for sugarin'," you say.

The girl squints up there. She still looks perplexed.

"You kin see pretty good from in there," Nat says. "There isn't any undergrowth, but the big trees'll hide you. I'll start up the road. You stay right in there till you see those hunters go by and then come back. Don't move till they're long gone."

"But how'll we catch up with you?" you ask.

"And what if someone sees us?" the girl asks.

Nat peers from one of you to the other. His gaze glints in the moonlight. "You'll have to come up this road on foot," he says, "but you can't let nobody see you. It's dangerous, but I can't see any other way. And Montpelier's still a long ways off."

Turn to page 45.

The woman made it this far north—she must know what she's doing. You decide to bring her the knife.

But first you've got to get one—somehow.

You scurry over to the Bates house. You knock at the back door. Zeb comes; his freckles lift into a smile.

"Thee has decided to help us?"

"Zeb," you say, breathless, "I got to do something first. I went to see the ones they caught. They need a knife."

"A . . . knife?"

"Yes. A sharp one. They need it to escape. Can you get me one? I mean, if you're going to help these folks now . . ."

But Zeb shakes his head.

"We are Friends," he says. "We cannot assist violence."

"But you don't have to."

"We cannot provide instruments of violence," Zeb says. "I'm sorry." He shrugs his shoulders. "We just cannot."

"Okay," you say. "It's all right. I'll see you shortly—I hope."

"May the light shine clear for thee," Zeb calls after you.

A few moments later, you're at your own back door. Your mother is busy in the kitchen. She has two knives in the kitchen—a small, sharp one and a larger one.

You can't wait until she's done. You've got to act now.

Turn to page 116.

You cross the tracks and walk through a field of tall corn across from the little house. There, in a second-story window above the back porch, you see a face peering out.

Now you know. And you're the only one who does.

It's just a few hours before the train comes. Maybe you should run and tell Henry Briggam, the millworker who vowed to confront the slave hunters. They'd storm this house for sure—and they're big, tough men. But so are the others, the ones who stood with Zachariah Gray. If they mean what they said, there could be trouble.

You could try to help the captives yourself—maybe wait for a chance to climb up onto the half roof above the back porch to the window where you saw the face. The quiet way might work. But if you're caught, you could go to jail. Helping a runaway slave is against the law.

If you run to tell the millworkers who oppose slavery, turn to page 11.

If you try to sneak the captives out yourself, turn to page 77.

"My God," one of the millworkers says.

A murmur rises as the men slowly surround the curled figure lying bloodied on the ground. Finally, one of his fellow workers kneels next to Gray and lifts his head.

The man looks up. "He's dead," he tells the workers.

There is only silence. You look up at the slave hunters' guard on the porch. He still grips his rifle, but his face is white.

"We'd best get help," one of the workers says.

"Yeah."

"The sheriff, I guess. Too late for the doc."

"And the wagon from the burial home."

"Yeah."

The men shuffle backward and awkwardly walk away.

Now only Henry Briggam is left standing over the body of the man he worked alongside just an hour ago.

He stoops to lift the axe handle. He looks down at it as if it's a thing he's never seen before. Now he turns and looks at you.

"You'd best go, too," he says. His voice is hollow and weak. "Go now."

You don't answer. There's nothing to say. As you start to walk back into town, you can't help looking back at the big man, a murderer now, standing helpless by the body and the blood.

Turn to page 37.

Something tells you your mother is right—the town's women must be told.

You dash from house to house, banging on doors and gasping out the news. One after another the women, both young and old, nod, wipe their hands, yank off their aprons, and stride or even run toward the railroad tracks.

Slab City is still a small town, and in a few minutes your alarm raising is done. Dashing for the hideaway house, you turn a corner and slide to a dusty stop.

Before you the crowd of antislavery men stands outside the door of the house that holds the captive slaves. Their faces are set, their hands on their hips.

In the street facing the men is the property-rights crowd, looking just as determined—and holding up clubs, shovels, and axes.

All the men look angry. They stare each other down—but they don't attack. They can't.

Between the two burly crowds weaves a thin line of smaller, shorter figures. Dressed in their plain cotton dresses, the town's women stand shoulder-to-shoulder. Some face the antislavers; some face the property men, arms folded.

Smack in the middle of the line you see your ma.

Turn to page 18.

You walk across town to the house where the captive slaves are being held. As you watch, the scruffy-looking slave hunter comes out on the front porch. He stares sternly at you. He's holding a rifle.

There seems to be nothing you can do for the people inside. Your choice is clear. You turn away.

When Zebediah opens his back door, his freckled face breaks into a quiet smile.

"Thee must join us, then," he says. "Come in."

Inside you're met with a sight even more startling than coming upon the eminent man in the front parlor—Loren Griswold sitting at the kitchen table. Mister Griswold is eating a pile of fresh, steaming doughnuts that Rebeccah Bates has placed on the table. The former state senator turns to acknowledge you.

"I am glad to see you," he says. "The new station will need your help. Please sit with us."

Wide-eyed, you draw back a chair and sit. Zeb does, too.

"The fewer souls who know of our work, the better," Griswold is telling the Bateses. "The proslavers are in every town. There are many among my fellow businesspeople, I am sad to say, who align themselves with those who traffic in human bondage."

Go on to the next page.

"As if one human being could ever own, buy, or sell another," Rebeccah declares.

"Exactly—but let the Anti-Slavery Society make that argument in public," Griswold cautions. "Our work is done more quietly. And it must resume tonight."

There's a soft knock at the back door.

Turn to page 93.

As the crowd disperses, you walk with your mother and father toward home.

"What you said to those men, Pa," you say, "it kinda surprised me."

"It's not our business to mind Southerners' affairs," he says. "If we do, this whole country's likely to go up in flames. But when folks start chaining up human beings in my town—that's *my* business."

Your mother takes your father's hand. "The slaves are human beings down there, too," she says gently.

Your father looks at the ground. Now he studies your ma.

"What's it worth to you to solve that problem?" he asks. "Will you send your own child for a soldier?"

Your mother stops dead. She looks at you. "Oh, I hope that's not what it's coming to," she says.

In the gentle Vermont summer evening, you, your mother, and your father go on walking toward your home.

Nine years in the future, in 1862, at Lee's Mills, Virginia, you will be a corporal in the Third Regiment of the Vermont Brigade when it is ordered to wade across a deep creek, straight at a line of Confederate riflemen. In the assault every second Vermont soldier will be wounded or killed. You'll be shot in the neck. You will fall and bleed to death in the warm water.

The End

It's still early afternoon when three men approach the *Herald* office. Two of them are scruffy looking, wearing threadbare country clothes, but the third is tall and wears a pale linen suit. That must be how a Southern gentleman dresses.

When a large enough reward has been offered, the slave hunters come north chasing runaways. The hunters must bring their captives back alive. Slaves are valuable, and the plantation owners are offering ever larger rewards in their campaign to stop the fast-growing traffic on the Underground Railroad.

The men step inside and come out moments later with a sheaf of broadsides. You peek around the corner.

"Hep, you post these notices all over town," the man in the suit is saying. "Carstairs, I want you at the hidin' place. I don't trust these Yankees."

"Right," the scruffy men say—and they walk together along the dusty main street. The man in the suit turns the other way, back toward the covered bridge.

You decide to follow the country guys. Soon they separate. The one called Hep begins to nail up the printed sheets on the doorframes of shops, one after another. Carstairs walks toward the railroad tracks.

You want to find the hiding place of the captive slaves—so you follow the second man. As you walk, you start to figure out their plan.

Turn to page 98.

Nat doesn't answer. He just stares ahead up the turnpike.

"Tell you what, old man," says the Southerner, leaning into Nat's face. "Why don't you just stare straight ahead like that. Just don't move, don't do a thing. We'll just rummage quickly through this pile of hay back here."

Slowly, Nat reaches under the wooden plank seat. He lifts an ancient flintlock pistol. He holds it up to Shelby Winton's nose.

"This wagon may not seem like much to you," Nat says, his voice even and steady, "but it's mine. We both live under the same laws, mister. And if you don't have a sheriff with a search warrant for this wagon, you'd be wise to get the hell away from it, and from me."

Gently, Winton lays one finger on the gun's barrel. He nudges it downward.

"A search warrant I can get—and I will," he says. "You won't get more than a mile before I'm back with the sheriff and that piece of paper. But then you'll have chosen jail—when right now, just by nodding toward the back, you could be choosing one hundred U.S. dollars."

Winton guides the pistol away from himself and leans forward again.

"What about it, old man? You've never seen this kind of money before in your life, and you never will again. That pile of hay may be yours, but the runaway underneath it is ours. Why not settle up here and now?"

Turn to page 88.

32

You just don't feel right about bringing back a knife. You're going to try your own idea instead.

But who in town has the tools that can take a bed apart? You think for a minute. Then you know.

You walk across town quickly but calmly. You cross the covered bridge and push open the door of the tavern stables.

Your friend the stable boy is still here. He's pitchforking hay to the horses.

"You work a long day, Dickey," you say, easing the big door closed.

"I guess I do," he says.

"There's no one else here, is there?"

"No," he says. "But I can't go fishin' with you, even so. I got to . . ."

"No—it's not that. I found those people."

"You mean the ones they caught? You found 'em?" Dickey's face is bright with curiosity.

"Yes, and I think I can get them away. But I need your help."

Dickey considers for a second. Then he goes to the wall and takes down another pitchfork.

"Here," he says, tossing it to you. "If I'm going to help you, you have to help me first. We got to get these horses fed for the night, and these stalls cleaned. If you help, we'll be done fast."

You start pitching hay. While you're working, you ask, "Dickey, can you take apart an iron bed?"

Turn to page 56.

Your senses alert as a squirrel's, you drop from Molly's back in the dark, empty barnyard. You walk to the barn door and pull.

It creaks slowly open. The moon casts a wedge of dusty light inside. In here you can see a small covered carriage, an old two-seater. But there's no commotion of farm animals. The barn is quiet.

Silently you draw the horse inside. Jubilee shuts the barn door behind you. You stroke the horse's neck in the darkness.

Before long the hoofbeats come drumming by along the road. They pull up before the house. You can hear the sound of voices out there, but you can't make out the words. The voices rise in argument.

"You won't disturb an old widow in the middle of the night," a man says sternly. That's the sheriff. "Now let's push on or turn back," he says. "Either one."

You hold your breath, hoping they'll turn back. But they don't. After a minute, the horses start up the turnpike again.

You sag in dismay.

"Looks like we got to spend the night here," you whisper to Jubilee.

But before she can answer, the big barn door creaks open. Lamplight enters through the crack. It's followed by the long, dark barrel of a gun.

Turn to page 55.

"Margery Griswold?"

"She was a Pequot Indian," Nat says. "Only daughter of the chief down to Chicopee, Mass. This was a hundred years ago. Young white man named Griswold, Joseph it was—he was traveling nearby when he got swept into the Connecticut River. About drowned. When his friends brought him into the Pequot village near the river, he wasn't well at all.

"Well, the chief's daughter was good with healing plants and such," the hill farmer says. "She nursed that fellow back to health. 'Course they was young and so forth, so they fell in love. The Griswold fellow's family opposed it, and so did the chief's—so naturally, they got married. Confounded 'em all.

"The story don't say how they came to Randolph Township, Vermont," Nat goes on, "but I figure folks that hardheaded just knew they belonged here. So they came. They had seven kids, and Margery was a healer. She had a white mare she'd ride to tend to anyone that was ailing. Didn't matter when nor where—she'd go.

"One winter night when Joseph and Margery had been married about fifty years—so she wa'n't no youngster anymore—there was a blizzard out, but a neighbor needed doctorin'. Margery wore out that white mare of hers, tryin' to get there. Borrowed another horse and wore that one out, too. So she set out on foot, in that kind of snow you can't see but three feet in front of you."

"What happened to her?" you ask.

Turn to page 90.

You're chasing a mob that's chasing a mob, and there's real trouble in the air. You dash across the covered bridge, but now you can only stand and watch as the property-rights men fill the main street of town, waving axes, shovels, and staffs.

Whatever's going to happen, you know you have to be there—you have to see it. You have an awful feeling that if it's bad, it'll be your fault.

People are standing in the doors of shops, watching with puzzled and fearful looks. You see your mother in the doorway of the *Herald*, wiping her hands.

You dash over.

"Ma—I found the captured slaves, in a house by the tracks, and I told the men! Now one crowd's bound to set them loose, and the other's bound to stop 'em. There's gonna be awful trouble."

Your mother peers at the dusty storm of men already moving fast toward the tracks.

"Listen," she says, "you and I have to round up the women."

"What? The *women*? Why?"

Turn to page 82.

Not long after, you're in the stable of the Mansion House Tavern, talking to Dickey as the stable hand shovels out an empty horse stall.

"What'll happen to those slaves?" Dickey asks. "The ones they caught?"

"I guess they're going back where they came from," you answer. "Everyone's talking about the murder now. There's even a judge in town. They took Henry to him, and now they're taking him to the jail."

Dickey shovels, silent, for a while. You just lean against the stall.

"What'll happen to us?" you ask.

"What do you mean?"

"I mean, if people are that fierce about all this—if they'll do that to each other," you say, "what'll happen to us?"

"I don't know—nothin', probably," says the stable boy.

In the years to come, your friend will survive the battles of First Bull Run, Antietam, and Fredericksburg, only to lose an arm to a Confederate cannonball when the Thirteenth Vermont Volunteers flank and shatter Pickett's Charge on the climactic and nightmarish final afternoon of the Battle of Gettysburg.

"Maybe tonight was the worst of it," Dickey says.

You set your chin on your fists. "Yeah," you say. "Maybe so."

The End

A midnight chase on horseback might be exciting, but it sounds like a good way to get caught. It's best, you decide, to lay low for a little bit until Winton Shelby and his scruffy sidekick give up. Then your path to Montpelier will be clear.

"I think we should get off and hide," you say to Nat.

"All right," he says, nodding. Nat urges the horses forward and draws the wagon to the side of the road.

"Let's do this quick, while nobody's lookin'," he says. He turns toward the pile of hay in back. "All right in there, miss—come on . . ."

But he's interrupted by a spasm of sneezing. The hay pile shakes and shivers as someone beneath it unleashes one sneeze after another. You can't help giggling, and Nat rolls his eyes—but now he leaps to the side of the wagon as the hay pile begins to fall apart. The old farmer dances about it, heaping handfuls of hay back on the pile.

The shuddering stops and so does Nat, looking relieved. But now "Aa . . . *CHOO!*" The whole pile collapses. Out from the base of the mess pokes a dark head, with hay-decorated pigtails and a sheepish smile.

"*Lord* I'm glad those men went away," says the girl, who's about your age. "I couldn't've held in that air one *second* longer."

Turn to page 75.

Your shadows angle across the dust as you and Dickey make your way to the depot. The moon is up, and the side street glows pale in its light.

"I'm a little dizzy," Dickey says. His voice is starting to sound thick and groggy.

"Let me help," you say.

The walk to the train station isn't long, but Dickey's feet are dragging when you finally get there. You push open the door, one arm around your friend.

Bill Dobbs looks around from his seat behind the window. He gets up and opens the ticket office door, a whale-oil lamp in his hand.

"My heavens, what's happened?" he asks.

The stationmaster has white hair, though he isn't old. His face is clean-shaven, he laughs easily, and his voice is mellow and kind. Since the railroad sent him to run Randolph Township's first station when the train arrived four years ago in 1849, he's become known as a good man— one who'll help anybody.

He is also very active in the local chapter of the Vermont Anti-Slavery Society.

You don't know this, but you tell him your story anyway. As he listens, his eyes turn sharp and fiery.

Turn to page 13.

You move closer until you're standing beneath the tiny back porch. To reach the captives, you've got to scale one of the narrow posts that hold up the little half roof above you. From the roof you'll be able to reach the window where you saw the shadowy form.

You peek up. The back hall and kitchen are dark. Whoever's guarding the captives—probably that scruffy slave hunter—seems, by the lamplight, to be in the front parlor. At least you hope that's where he is.

You crouch. Reach up and grab the post. Start—as quietly as you can—to shinny up. Don't slip—don't fall off!

Up . . . up. Reaching, grabbing, holding on, you get a hand on the half roof. Don't slip— hold on. . . . You catch your breath, grip hard with both legs, and reach up with the other hand. It scrabbles for a hold—slips off. You reach up again. You've got it.

Now, push up with your clamped knees, and pull with all your strength. Your head is above the roof. You're grunting, squirming up, your palms on the roof now, pushing yourself up. Soft as you can, breathing hard but quietly, you heave yourself up onto the roof.

There's a scrabbling in the dark room next to you. You look up quickly. A face appears in the shadows of the window. You can almost see the features. Whoever it is can *definitely* see you.

Turn to page 50.

Your mother stiffens as your father stamps into the kitchen. He's a big, bearded man. Inside his shirt, his shattered shoulder is wrapped tightly to his body.

"Loren Griswold and his damned abolitionists," your father growls. "They're up there on that hill thinking they're better than us down here. They don't need money 'cause they already grabbed all of what's around here. *Now* they figure they got the right to tell Southern folks what to do with their property."

This is a familiar tirade. Your mother scrapes at the sizzling fish. You stare straight ahead, knowing what your father does not know—about what has happened.

The pain he is in makes him angry. Your father is a sawyer, a man of some authority in the mill—he ran the big blade. But several weeks ago the blade flung back a knotty slab and smashed his shoulder. Now he lives with the humiliation of having to stay home while his wife works, setting type at the town newspaper and printing shop, to keep your family alive. It makes him angry.

Turn to page 52.

Samuel Bates only needs to look at his wife for a moment. He turns back to Loren Griswold, his gentle voice sure.

"Thee have come to the right place. We see the way clear."

"Then you'll help? The need is immediate," Griswold says.

"We will surely help," Rebeccah says.

"But the risk is genuine," Griswold cautions. "The Fugitive Slave Act has . . ."

"There are higher laws than that one," Samuel says.

"I quite agree, Samuel, I quite agree. Well, then—it's settled. Your next station is in Montpelier, at the office of the *Voice of Freedom*. Joseph Poland, the editor, is an ardent supporter of our cause.

"But the trip to Montpelier is long, dark, and difficult—especially now," he goes on. "Tonight's cargo has, for some reason, a sizable reward attached to its capture and safe return. The mercenaries are searching in a rather frenzied manner."

"Where is the . . . cargo?" Rebeccah asks.

"It will be delivered to you after dark," Griswold says.

Turn to page 9.

You nod and hustle the girl off the road. Pushing through some brambles that scratch at your legs, you climb together into the sugarbush.

You hide behind a big tree. You watch the turnpike as the cart disappears over a rise. Now, coming from the other direction, you hear hooves.

"Didn't take 'em long," you say.

The girl nudges you. She asks, "What's sugarin'?"

You blink at her. Stalks of hay still stick out from her pigtails. This girl has been hidden in whiskey barrels and been eaten by bugs—and who knows what else—and now the slave hunters are coming again. And she wants to ask *questions*?

"It's makin' sugar from maple sap," you whisper. "Comes from these trees—in the springtime."

The girl gazes upward in wonder. "Sugar from *trees*?" she whispers. "I declare."

"*Shh.*" You nudge her. Two riders have come into view.

Turn to page 6.

Lamplight plays on the faces of the five men as they stand abreast, blocking the way to the tracks. As the train's heavy chugging nears and its whistle sounds again, the slave hunter studies the men.

The minister, Reverend Jackson, steps forward.

"Sir," he says, "we are the local chapter of the Vermont Anti-Slavery Society. You are welcome to get on this train and leave our town—but these two people are not going with you."

"Oh no?" The hunter draws a small pistol from beneath his shirt. The train clatters closer.

"And which of you," he says, "is ready to take a bullet for two slaves?"

All five men step forward.

The hunter blinks.

"Choose anyone," the minister says. "You've only got one shot. Then, of course, you'll spend your life in prison."

"In a *Yankee* prison," adds the burly black-smith Hawke.

Turn to page 57.

"We come from a Tidewater plantation—a pretty big one," Jubilee finally says. "Our master's name is Peter Horn. He ain't a bad man, especially for a slave master. He treated us all right. But he was in love with my momma."

"With your *momma*? Isn't that who got caught in the Center last night?"

"Yes—my little brother, too," Jubilee says. "Master Horn told my momma if we ever tried to run off north, he'd see to it we were caught—he'd hire the best slave catchers around. And then he'd sell my brother and me south."

"Sell you south? What's that mean?"

"It means we never see Momma again, for one," she says. "Slaves that get sold south usually get worked to death, or worse."

"So then why'd your momma run?"

There's another silence. The hoofbeats behind you are closer now.

"I can't explain it," the girl says. "You ain't been—"

"Shush!" You glance behind. "Those horses are gonna catch up! Why'd we ever think we could outrun those men?"

"*You* shush," Jubilee says. "Look up there."

A run-down, unpainted house stands ahead. Clapboards are falling off it. It looks abandoned. Behind it is a small barn.

"Think we can hide in there?" Jubilee says.

"We got to try," you answer.

Turn to page 34.

The scream . . . that was Dickey!

You hear a clatter as the slave hunter drops his rifle. You run to the window in time to see him cross the tracks and plunge into the cornfield.

You call out, "Dickey!"

"Yeah," answers the stable boy. His voice is coming from across the tracks. You can't see him, but you can hear his heavy panting.

"Are you hurt bad?"

"I don't know," the boy says. "It's just my arm, but it's bleeding."

You run downstairs. You know why your friend was shot and not the others—because slaves are valuable. If the hunter shoots either the woman or her little boy, he will lose the bounty on their return. By shooting Dickey instead he has cut down their helper and terrified the runaways, too.

So now your friend is hurt—maybe badly. He needs your help.

But somewhere in that dark cornfield, the man can hear the clanking of the fugitives' chain. Without that chain, the woman and her child might very easily lose him in the corn. But with all that noise they're going to be run down and caught—unless you can do something.

Whom do you help first: your friend who's hurt because of you? Or the runaway slaves who'll be caught without your help?

---

*If you try to help the runaways,
turn to page 8.*

*If you try to help your friend first,
turn to page 73.*

50

For a long moment you crouch there, frozen on the roof. But there's only one way to go: forward.

You rise and pad on bare feet to the window sash. The face is there, inside the lightless room. The person can't seem to come to the window, but it's there, just a few feet away.

You peer and blink, trying to see. There's someone else in there, too. Someone small.

The closer, larger figure retreats to the smaller one, as if to protect it.

"Who are you?" it asks.

Her voice—it's definitely a woman—is low but steady. She sounds as if she's already seen the worst that could happen.

"I'm a friend," you whisper. "I'm from the village. I want to help you."

The woman seems to turn toward the room's closed door for a moment.

"Come in," she murmurs. "Quick."

You swing your legs through the window and set your feet silently on the floor.

Your eyes are more used to the light now so you can see them better: a young, very beautiful black woman and a large-eyed little boy. You stand there staring at them.

Finally you whisper, "Come on—let's get out of here. I'll go first. Then I can help you climb . . ."

"Can't," the young woman says.

She holds up her arm to show you why.

Turn to page 107.

"High-and-mighty abolitionists aren't above the law any more than we are," he says. "They've got no right to interfere with the Southerners' legal business—no right to tell them or anyone else what to do. When I got hurt, did Loren Griswold care? Of course not! You think he cares any more about some colored folk? He doesn't! He just wants to feel he's better than us. Well, he isn't—and he is not above the law. If he gets caught he'll go to jail like anyone else."

But your excitement is growing. Loren Griswold may be the richest man in the whole Township of Randolph—will he *really* go to jail? And where are the captured runaway slaves?

You've got to find out. While your father is still grumbling and your mother's face is still flushed, you're out the back door.

Turn to page 105.

But no one invites you to speak—so of course you stay silent.

"There is no possibility, at least for the immediate future, that I can continue in the role in which I have been honored to serve," Mister Griswold tells Samuel and Rebeccah Bates.

"These mercenaries, these hirelings of the slave owners, have invaded my home and discovered certain secret places within it. Now my home is no longer a safe and secure refuge for those who need our help.

"In fact," Mister Griswold continues, "though there are others in the Center who are quite willing to take over our duties, I feel strongly that, at least for the present, my own village is not secure. More of these slave hunters will be descending on us, hoping to search out their human quarries in our midst."

"We quite understand thee," Samuel Bates says. Rebeccah nods. In most homes, you know—Loren Griswold's included—the wife would not be admitted to such an important conversation. But the Quakers are different.

"This, then, is why I believe the station must migrate elsewhere in our township," Griswold says. "This village is away from the turnpike—and you, Samuel and Rebeccah, are Friends. In this time of urgent need, I must turn to you. Please forgive my haste, but I must ask you directly: will you take over this work?"

Turn to page 44.

A tall, thin, elderly woman steps into the barn. She holds the lamp in one hand. The gun is crooked in her other arm. Standing next to Jubilee, you peek from behind the horse.

"All right, I see a horse," the woman whispers. "Who else? Come out, now—I can shoot this thing, and I will."

You step from behind the horse. The woman's brow creases when she sees you. Now Jubilee steps from behind you.

The woman's face turns angry.

"I don't know what you two young people figure on doing in my barn, but you figured wrong," she says. "Just because I'm an old . . ."

Jubilee unties her bonnet. She takes it off.

The woman's voice trails off. She holds up the lantern, peering at the girl's face.

Now she sets the gun down. She walks forward and slips her hand in Jubilee's.

"Come with me," she says. "It's all right. I won't tell."

Turn to page 89.

"Sure," the stable boy says. "But why do you need to take a bed apart?"

"Because these two folks are chained to it. Do we need tools?"

Dickey doesn't answer. He opens a big wooden box and draws out a black iron wrench.

"This should do the job," he says, smiling.

Soon you're back on the half porch in the dark, having shinnied up the pole once more. You grip the roof's edge with one hand and lean over as far as you dare while Dickey reaches up on tiptoes. He holds the wrench straight up. You hold your breath, hoping the back door doesn't open.

Your fingers close on the wrench. You grab it and pull yourself up. Dickey scurries back and hides behind a tree.

The woman and her little boy watch you swing in the window. The door to the bedroom is still shut.

"Did you bring the knife?" she asks.

"No," you say. "Listen. You've got to trust me. I've got a plan."

She looks at the floor a moment. Then she shrugs.

"I been trustin' white folks ever since we crossed the Mason-Dixon Line," she says. "It don't seem natural, but I guess I got to keep on doin' it. What you got in mind?"

You hold up the wrench. "If I can just get a couple of bolts off this bed," you say, "without making any noise . . ."

Turn to page 114.

The locomotive's headlamp lights the side of each man's face. With thunderous clanking, the train draws in. Its brakes wheeze and screech as it slows to a stop.

The white-haired stationmaster steps between the hunter and the village men.

"You've got your ticket," Bill Dobbs says to the man in his kindly way. "Why not step on the train?"

For almost a minute, the man doesn't move. The train's two passenger cars are lit a soft yellow from inside.

The slave hunter drops the chain. He shoves the derringer beneath his shirt. The men of the Anti-Slavery Society part ranks to let him step through, and he boards the train, alone.

The End

"Nat, those were the slave catchers. They were watching us."

"Imagine they watch everyone goes through town," Nat says.

"Have slave catchers ever stopped you—tried to search the wagon?"

"Never have," Nat says. His flinty face stares forward. "Like to see 'em try."

"Well," you say, "I hear horses back there."

Nat's expression doesn't change, and he doesn't look back. But the sound of horses grows nearer. Before long, as you travel the old ridgetop turnpike, two horses with riders crest the rise behind you. They easily overtake your plodding wagon.

The man in the pale suit draws his horse across your path. Expressionless, his sharp face set, Nat pulls in the reins.

"Hello there, old gentleman," the Southerner smoothly says, nodding to Nat and ignoring you. "My name is Winton—Shelby Winton."

"Evenin'," Nat says.

"I happen to be looking for a certain piece of stolen property," the man says. "Now, it could be that someone who's come into possession of this property might not realize that it rightly belongs to someone else."

Nat does not answer.

Go on to the next page.

"What's more," the man continues, "there's quite a sizable reward involved. One hundred dollars, simply for information that leads to the recovery of this property."

Shelby Winton reaches in his jacket pocket. He pulls out a packet of bills and holds it up to Nat's pinched face.

"A hardworking man like you could use this," he says. "Let us look in that hay pile there, and it's yours."

The Southerner leans back. He smiles. "That's all there is to it," he says.

Turn to page 31.

The man sends for the sheriff, who follows the path of pushed-over cornstalks into the field. It's midmorning when he finds your body and suspects instantly who killed you. But by then the slave hunter and his bounty have long since switched trains at White River Junction and are almost to New York.

The Fugitive Slave Act is on the hunter's side—and because of it no one else tries to interfere during their three days' train ride across the Mason-Dixon Line, back into the world of slavery.

The End

You see the lamplight flicker inside the house as the guard leaves the front parlor. The lamp moves upstairs.

The upper room's dimness goes yellow with oil-fired light, and as it does a woman's voice speaks sharply. There's a clatter of irons. A man's husky voice answers harshly and you hear a heavy clanking. Something metal clangs to the ground. You hear the sound of glass shattering.

The light in the room surges and turns red and orange.

It's on fire. The lamp must have broken!

You break from the field and rush to the house. As you jump up on the porch the man's boots pound down the stairs. He hurtles out the door. His eyes are wild with panic. They fasten on you.

"Kid! Kid! This town's got a fire brigade, don't it?"

"Yeah."

"Then *go get 'em*! They's two slaves up there—worth hundreds of dollars!"

"Can't we get 'em out?"

"No! They's chained up, and they's fire all around! *Run!*"

Turn to page 99.

There's no time to go rounding up women—and what good could that do anyway? You've got to get to where the captured slaves are being held, and where the millworkers are headed.

The antislavers have reached the house first. The scruffy-looking slave catcher whose job it is to guard the captives inside stands on the porch. He grips a rifle, looking uncertain.

Henry Briggam, the tall millworker who led the antislavers here, stands at the head of his crowd as the property-rights men come stomping toward the house. Briggam's strong arms are folded across his chest.

You run around to get a good look. The property-rights men move threateningly toward the antislavers, scowling and gripping their long-handled tools.

Zachariah Gray, the stocky leader of the property-rights men, steps up to Briggam. Gray is holding his double-edged lumberman's axe. Both its ends are sharpened to a gleam.

"I see you boys brought your toys," Henry says, glaring at Zachariah.

"Bet you wish you did the same, right about now," the bearded man answers with a smile.

"Listen, you scraggly blowhard," says Henry. "The people inside here are human beings—same as me and same as you, more or less. You're on the wrong side of this."

"Try me, then," Zachariah challenges. "Make one move toward that house and see what side you'll be on."

Turn to page 86.

"Ma," you begin, "they're bound with a rope. I can get to 'em, Ma—I already have. All I have to do is cut that rope. That's all I need the knife for. Then I can sneak them out. Ma, I know how you feel about slavery. These folks are just like regular people—I swear they are. I got to help them, Ma."

Your mother sits on a bench, erect and still. She doesn't answer.

"I got to do it *now*, Ma. Please. It's just to cut the rope."

A tear rolls down your mother's face. But she remains perfectly still. She stares straight ahead and does not turn or look at you as you stand up and slowly walk back into the kitchen.

When you come out, the knife is in your hand. With your other hand you carefully let the door shut behind you. Your mother still stares straight ahead, tears flowing down her face.

You slip the knife into your trousers and set off at a dead run. You only hope there's enough time.

Turn to page 91.

It's a long, bumpy, bone-wearying night's ride. The earliest gray of dawn is just a hint over the tall hills when your carriage finally creaks down the streets of Montpelier, Vermont's capital city and a northern hub of the Underground Railroad.

Citizens boldly point out the office of the *Voice of Freedom*, the abolitionist newspaper published by the outspoken Joseph Poland. He lives upstairs from his office, in a white frame home on State Street.

Though you've woken him up and he's never seen you before, Joseph Poland—a young, clean-shaven man with dancing bright *eyes*—throws open his front door.

"Come in, come in—most glad you've arrived," he says.

In his kitchen he serves the three of you doughnuts and coffee. You tell him about the slave hunters.

"We saw no sign of 'em last night," you say, "but they're out there still, that's for sure."

"They won't come *here*," Poland says. "And we'll get you across the border as safe as can be," he tells Jubilee with a grin. "The farther north you go, the more ornery Vermonters get. There's not one person working on the line from here to Canada that won't stand up to those lowlifes."

Mrs. Flint nudges you. "It's time we started home," she says softly.

Turn to page 111.

The guard is coming! There's only one thing you can think of to do.

"Go to the edge and jump," you tell the woman. "Quick! Dickey, here they come! Get 'em out of here!"

The woman grabs her boy, and the heavy chain drags and rattles as she hurries to the roof's edge.

But you can't stay to watch. You turn and scuttle back across the dark floor to the pieces of iron bedstead. Feeling among them in the dimness, you come up with the heavy wrench. The footsteps are at the door now. You crouch beside it.

Rifle in one hand, lantern in the other, the slave catcher kicks the door open, shoving you into the corner on the other side.

You didn't think of that.

The guard scans the room quickly. Before you can think of what to do he's running back down the stairs.

You hear him throw open the front door.

"You stop!" he shouts. "I'll shoot! I will!"

A rifle shot cracks in the night. You hear a scream from across the tracks.

Turn to page 49.

Nat releases one of the horses from the wagon harness. He pulls a leather bridle from beneath his seat and fits it on.

"This is Molly," he says. "She ain't so fast, and you'll have no saddle, I'm sorry to say."

Nat boosts you up onto the horse's soft brown back. The girl follows. The farmer steps back, hands on his hips. Now he shakes his head.

"This'll never do," he says. "There's no dark folks in Vermont to speak of—and you ridin' up there, plain to see . . . You'll never make it."

The girl reaches into a small burlap sack hung around her waist. She pulls out a very large flowered bonnet and ties it around her chin. It's so huge her face is swallowed inside.

It looks ridiculous, but Nat only nods.

"That's some better, 'cept for the hands." The girl's dark hands stick out from the too-short sleeves of her rough boy's shirt.

Nat begins to unbutton his own checked farmer's shirt. He pulls it off. Like all Vermont farmers, he's wearing long-sleeved woolen underwear beneath, even in the summertime. He hands his shirt up to the girl.

She puts it on. The long sleeves dangle past her hands. With the bonnet, the huge shirt, and the cut-off trousers, she looks like a clown—but her skin is hidden.

"I don't understand white folks," the girl sighs. "Some'll work you to death, others give you their shirt." She shakes her head.

You hear hoofbeats.

Turn to page 78.

You swallow. "A knife?"

She nods. "It don't have to be big. Just sharp. Bring it quick."

"But . . . what are you going to do with it?"

"Ain't goin' to use it if I don't have to," she says. "Now if you want to help, *bring me a knife*."

She sits down on the bed.

"We'll wait," she says, and glances at her son. Utterly silent, the little boy still watches you with big eyes.

You nod unsurely and back up, feeling behind you for the windowsill. Touching it, you turn and loop one leg out. Then you turn back.

But the woman only stares. She nods, as if to say, *Do it*. You slip onto the porch.

You drop with a soft thud to the ground.

Inside the house, footsteps thump your way.

You fall below the back porch level. The back door creaks open. A lamp's gleam plays just over your flattened body. It flickers across the yard.

"Hmph," the man growls. His boots thump back. The door creaks again, and it's dark and silent.

Go on to the next page.

Should you bring the knife? What will she do with it if she has to? You don't know. Maybe you should just trust her and follow her directions.

But maybe not. What do the Quakers call it— waiting for the light? An idea is dawning in your head.

With the right tool, *those beds come apart.* And the right tool for that purpose is not a knife.

What should you go after: the knife or the tool?

If you go for the knife, turn to page 21.

If you go for the tool, turn to page 32.

In a moment you're at Dickey's side. You strip off your shirt and bind it around his wounded arm. The wound doesn't seem deep, but it's bleeding badly.

The cornfield rises just behind you. All is still for the moment. Maybe both hunter and slaves are listening for each other.

"I want to go after them," you say.

But Dickey shakes his head.

"Don't just blunder in there," he says. "What if he has a knife or something?"

"Hmm." You nod. "All right, then," you whisper. "Come on."

"Where to?"

You incline your head back toward the empty house. He nods. You help your friend over the tracks and onto the porch.

"There's no water, I don't think," you tell Dickey as you lay him gently down.

"It's okay," he says, pushing your hand aside with his good arm. "I'm not so bad."

But you shake your head, looking at his arm. The cloth is already soaked with blood.

"Got to find you some help," you mutter. "Where can we get to quickly?"

Dickey looks up at you.

"The railroad depot," he says. "Bill Dobbs'll be there—the train's almost due."

Go on to the next page.

He's right. Bill Dobbs is the stationmaster. But what about the runaways?

You look across the tracks. From the cornfield comes a quick crackling sound, like someone pushing through the stalks. A woman cries out. You hear clanking. Then nothing.

"They're caught," you whisper. "I know they are."

Turn to page 40.

The girl sits up. She perches on the wagon's edge, picking hay from a cotton smock and a pair of very baggy trousers, much too big for her and cut off at the knee. Meanwhile Nat darts around, comically heaping back handfuls of hay on the wagon, trying to build back the pile.

"You two git to helpin' me!" he says to the girl, looking sharply at you both. "Those fellas see hay all over, they're going to know just what happened."

The girl looks at you and hops off the wagon. All three of you work hurriedly in the night.

"Got to clean every last bit off this road," Nat says, straightening up and watching the two of you finish the job. "I got to admit, though, you did all right holdin' that sneezin' in so long."

The girl grins again. Her smile is lopsided; bits of hay stick out all over her head. She looks kind of like a clown, but she doesn't tell clown stories.

"That wasn't the worst," the girl says. "Once I was hid in an empty whiskey barrel. It was so bad smellin' I got dizzy and sick. And the *headache* I had next day, Lord it was awful.

"Other time I spent a whole night's ride hidin' under a buffalo robe that was *crawlin'* with bugs," she said. "Had to let 'em bite me the whole night long. Couldn't move or nothin'. I can still feel those little pincers all over.

"I guess since we started north, this hay was third worst," she says.

"Enough talkin'," Nat warns. "Those men'll be comin' back."

Turn to page 20.

"What?" you ask.

Your mother looks nervously toward the inner house where your father is.

"I don't want him to hear this," she whispers. "You know how he feels about it."

"About *what*?"

She leans down. "About the railroad."

You look toward the tracks, across town. "About the . . ."

"Not *that* railroad," she hisses.

"Oh. The one that goes through the Center?" You're grinning with mischief—but your mother is not.

She nods. "I suppose you know—you seem to find out everything—that Mister Griswold's home has been the station, up in the Center. Last night a party of slave hunters came there with the sheriff. They'd got a search warrant, so the sheriff had to cooperate, and the Griswolds had to let them in. They found a secret room in the cellar. They captured a mother . . . and a little boy."

Your mother's face is dark with anger.

"It's worse than a crime," she says. "For those poor people to have come all this way . . ." She shakes her head and goes back to the stove.

But your curiosity is far from satisfied. There's so much else you want to know. How did the slave hunters find the secret station? Where did they take the fugitives?

"What'll happen to Mister Griswold?"

"*Griswold!*" Your father's voice explodes like an angry bear's.

Turn to page 42.

You decide to investigate on your own—to climb onto that back half porch, if you can do it, and find out if the captive slaves are really in there. What do slaves *look* like? You've never seen one before.

Maybe you should have some help. Somebody's got to boost you onto the porch and serve as lookout. The obvious choice is Zebediah Bates, your best friend.

But will Zeb do it? Helping a runaway slave is a crime. Then again, Zeb is a Quaker—and everyone knows that some Quaker families in Vermont, and many others elsewhere, have been risking arrest, fines, and prison to help the runaways. The Bates family has not been involved so far. But until now the Underground Railroad has bypassed Slab City, so there's been no need.

Now there's a need. You decide to go tell Zeb he's going to help.

But when Zeb comes to his back door, he's got a surprise for you.

"I must talk with thee," he says, as if he's been expecting you. "Come inside quickly."

Turn to page 17.

Nat glances back at the sound.

"This road goes straight to Montpelier," he says, "but it'll take you all night to get there. Don't stop for nothin' or nobody. Once there, go to the office of the *Voice of Freedom* newspaper. The editor is Mister Joseph Poland. He's the man you want.

"Once you're in Montpelier, you're safe," Nat says. "Folks there don't take to slave hunters at all. But till you get there, don't trust nobody—unless you have to."

He studies you and shakes his head.

"Don't like this," he says. "Don't like it at all."

"I'll get your horse back, Nat," you say.

"That'd be fine," he says. "But you get to Montpelier first."

He slaps Molly's flank. She sets off at a trot along the pale turnpike. You still hear hoofbeats behind you in the darkness.

"I wonder if Nat'll slow 'em up," you say.

"I bet he'll try," the girl says. Her arms hold on tight to you.

"What's your name?" you ask.

"Jubilee."

"What kind of name is that?"

"It stands for the freedom day," she says, "when we all get our freedom. That's what we call the Jubilee."

"How come there's such a big reward for you?"

For a long moment, there's silence. You can hear the horses drumming after you.

Turn to page 48.

80

Summer dust puffs around your feet as you run to the narrow wood office of the *Green Mountain Herald*. You slip in the back door.

Alone in the dim press room, your mother stands at a high, flat table. She's fitting metal type into a wide, shallow wooden tray. Her face is traced with tears.

"Ma—what is it?"

Shaking her head, she waves at the tray. "This is a broadside, a poster for another runaway slave," she says. Her voice is quavering. "They say I have to set it in type—it's my job! I have to keep my job."

"I thought they caught the fugitives," you say.

"They caught two—but apparently there's a third. A girl. She must have stayed hidden somehow, or slipped away when the hunters came. The reward for helping them catch her is a hundred dollars. Why so much—for a girl?"

You don't say anything.

"Why do I have to help them?" your mother says. "It's wrong, what they do."

You nod. "It's not your fault, Ma. It's *not*. Say, when will this broadside be printed?"

"Those men said they need it fast," she says. "They'll be back in an hour—less, now." She returns to the work. Her fingers shake as she fits type into the tray.

You slip out the door. In an alley a few feet from the *Herald*'s front door, you hug the shadows and wait.

Turn to page 30.

If you don't try to help the captives, no one else will. No one else knows where they are.

You glance back at Zeb's home. The lamps are burning inside. They've found their own light, as the Quakers say. Now it seems like you've found yours.

In the deepening gloom of the late summer evening, you make your way quietly to the railroad tracks at the upper edge of the village. Across the tracks is the field of tall corn. You walk along the tracks to a point just before you can be spotted from the house with the captive slaves. You slip into the corn.

The corn rustles. You feel as if it's crackling loud enough to be heard across town, let alone in the little white house you're approaching.

But there's no activity there that you can see. The home has been empty lately. It's perfect for the slave hunters' needs—vacant and right above the railroad station. In about an hour, when the train makes its evening stop, they'll be able to slip the captives down the dark street and onto a rail carriage undetected.

Or so they must think.

The downstairs is weakly lit by a single lamp. There's no light upstairs. But as you watch the house, looking for what to do next, you notice a shadow pass by the upstairs window.

Turn to page 41.

"Don't ask questions," your mother orders, "just go to the houses around your school. Pound on as many doors as you can. Tell the women what's going on."

"But why?"

"Just do it! I'll take this part of town. Now run!"

You run across the street and up an alley toward the crowd of homes behind the business area. But now you stop. Why tell the women—what can they do? Maybe stop the trouble somehow. But how?

You don't want to disobey your ma—but a powerful urge, spurred by dread and fascination, tells you to hotfoot it to the trackside house. Something's going to happen there, and soon.

But maybe doing as your ma told you is the only way to stop it.

If you help round up the town's women, turn to page 25.

If you run to the house where the men are going, turn to page 64.

"Nat Woodard has conducted many, many passengers to the next station," Loren Griswold tells you. "And though he's a flinty soul, these nighttime journeys are long and exhausting. Since the passage of the new Fugitive Slave Act, traffic through our station has been growing at a very fast pace. Two, three times a week, sometimes more, we must see to it that a 'parcel' is transported to Montpelier.

"Now we have a new station, and new stationmasters," Griswold says. He nods at Rebeccah, who's working at the kitchen counter. "We need more conductors.

"We'd like you to accompany Nat and our cargo on this journey," he says to you. "You are young, and your presence may help deflect suspicion. In time, perhaps soon, we may need you to conduct journeys on your own.

"If you go with Nat tonight, you won't get any sleep," Griswold says, "and the slave hunters are out there. It's hard to ask anyone to make the journey, but I must ask you. Will you go?"

You look from Griswold to Zeb, and up at Rebeccah. She glances your way.

"It is thine own light that thee must follow," she cautions. "Please decide for thyself."

"Yes, indeed," Griswold nods, and now he smiles as you hear a creaking sound outside. "But please decide quickly! I believe Nat's wagon is ready to begin."

Turn to page 108.

The men who side with Henry Briggam in hating slavery storm up the riverbank, their voices loud and fists shaking. They set off in a crowd toward town.

Among the men who are left, there's confusion for a moment. But now Zachariah Gray, the stocky workman, raises a shout of his own.

"Those men aim to interfere with people's rightful property," he thunders. "Men, if they do that, your own property could be next! Who's ready to fight for the American right of ownership?" He runs back to the mill and comes out with a double-bladed axe.

"If we let 'em steal a Southerner's slave today, what will they take of *yours* tomorrow?"

Other men crowd into the mill. They come out with axes, shovels, and the wooden staffs they use to push logs toward the blade.

"Let's go show 'em what stealing costs!" one man shouts.

"Property rights or no rights!" yells another.

You're looking at an armed mob.

The mob storms past you and up over the riverbank.

Turn to page 36.

"This ain't gonna stop here," the antislaver Henry Briggam tells Zachariah Gray.

Gray steps even closer to his adversary. He raises the two-bladed axe.

"*You*'ll stop here," he says. "I'll see to that. And those slaves will go back to their rightful owner, with no interference from your crowd."

"Just how much do you think a plantation owner in Maryland or Virginia cares about your loyalty to his precious property?" Briggam demands.

"It's a matter of *principle*," Gray shouts in Henry's face.

"I'll show you principle!"

The rangy antislaver's fist slams into Zachariah's face. The stocky man stumbles backward. His friends steady him, and he swings the big axe broadside, its flat side arcing at the tall man.

But Henry dodges the blow. He grabs the axe handle and wrenches it so hard that Zachariah stumbles and loses his grip. The stocky man roars in rage and charges Henry, his dark head down. Henry rears back and swings the axe in a wide, sideways path. The axe head buries into the side of Zachariah Gray.

The dark man drops to the ground. Henry Briggam releases the axe handle slowly and lets it fall. Everyone stands frozen, watching as dark blood spreads beneath the property-rights man in a thick pool.

Turn to page 24.

Nat doesn't say a word. He lifts the reins and shakes them. His two horses start forward.

You turn and smile at the two Southerners. They don't smile back.

"You won't get *half* a mile before I'll be on you with a search warrant," Shelby Winton promises. "Say good-bye to your wagon, your farm, everything! You're going to *jail*!"

The two men draw their horses around and spur them into the night, back toward the Center.

Turn to page 112.

Just after nightfall the next evening, you lead Molly out of Grace Flint's dusty barn. This time, though, Nat's horse is harnessed to Mrs. Flint's old covered carriage.

Mrs. Flint and Jubilee stand at the back door of the old cabin, watching you struggle to get the carriage ready.

"It's a creaky old thing, but it'll get us there," Mrs. Flint says. "Now let's climb up and get started."

Turn to page 113.

"Well, she made it," Nat says.

"In the snow?"

"Yep. Did her doctorin'. Next day Margery had pneumonia. It finished her. She's buried up here in the Center somewhere. No one knows exactly where."

"Was Loren Griswold one of her children?"

"Margery and Joseph was Loren's grandparents," Nat says. "And if you ask me, I'd say that's why he does what he does for these folks. It's in his blood to help. Don't matter if they got nothin', don't matter what color they be. Color don't make a person different anyhow, far as I've figured out. These runaways"—he nods back toward the hay pile—"they've seen plenty white-skinned stinkers, I guarantee you that."

Your wagon has crested the hill. You're creaking along the wide, straight central avenue of the village. Fine homes in brick and white paint line both sides.

As you pass one of the two Center taverns, a man in a pale suit steps out on the porch. He peers at your wagon and intently watches you go by.

Turning to look back, you see the man call into the door of the inn. Now that scruffy-looking guy has come onto the porch. The two slave hunters stand there, watching your wagon travel north.

Turn to page 59.

Several tense minutes later, you're at the second-floor window again. You hold up the knife so the moonlight catches its blade.

The woman—you don't know her name, nor her little boy's—only nods. You reach down and skitter the knife across the floor. She catches it and slips it into her skirt. She sees you looking at the skirt, and she looks down. It's a pretty patterned one.

"Lady give me this," she says. "Somewhere on the way. White lady. Never knew there was decent white people in the world."

She looks up at you.

"Go now," she says.

"I can stay," you say. "I can hide—and help."

She shakes her head. "You go."

Reluctantly, you nod. "Okay. I'll wait outside. Once you get out, I'll get you to a hiding place."

"*No*. You get as far from here as you can. You go home."

"What? But why?"

Her eyes are fierce.

"You just go home."

Not understanding, you climb down the porch post and slip across the tracks into the cornfield.

Hidden there, you stare at the little white house. It looks so ordinary. It's quite dark out here. The train should be along soon. The slave catchers will have to make their move. You wonder when the young woman will make hers.

Turn to page 62.

You whirl around, but Rebeccah Bates goes calmly to open the door.

In steps a stooped and angular man wearing a farmer's coarse clothes. The man removes his hat, and you recognize his skinny face, darkened and creased by weather and the years.

"I don't know if you've met Nathaniel Woodard," Loren Griswold says. He stands beside the lean man, who grips his hat and looks shyly down at the floor. The two men couldn't look more different. Griswold is portly and prosperous in a frock coat, while Nat Woodard is as scrawny and poor as the rocky soil he farms, way up in the hills above town.

Samuel Bates stands and shakes Nat's hand. "Please sit with us, Nathaniel," he says. The farmer perches on a chair like an uneasy bird.

"Our most unflinching friends are in our hills, among the hardscrabble farmers like the Woodards," Griswold says. "Nat's father fought the British with Ethan Allen, among the Green Mountain Boys. The Vermont hill farmer does not take the issue of freedom lightly."

"That package is in your barn, Mister Bates," Nat says to the Quaker. "I be 'bout ready to start for the market. If ye don't mind, I'll be loadin' my wagon."

"I'll come with you," Bates says. The two men go out to the barn.

Now Griswold turns to you. "You've likely wondered why we have included you in our tiny group," he says.

Turn to page 83.

Then, not far away, you hear something. It's gentle yet unmistakable: a soft clinking. As you stand very still, you hear it again. There's a slight rustling along with it, as the woman tries as quietly as she can to move away.

Don't do it, you think. *Don't move!* If they do, the hunter can follow the sound.

Nearby comes a heavy rustling. It's plunging toward the sound you just heard.

There's nothing else you can do now but get there, too. You start shoving cornstalks aside, moving as fast as you can in the direction of the clinking sound that's all but drowned out now by the rustling of cornstalks in your ears.

You're pushing this way, now more to the other side. Where *was* that sound? It's impossible to tell—there are no landmarks, no paths. And you're not an experienced hunter. But the other man is.

You hear a muffled curse and a woman's sharp cry. A quick shuffling sound is followed by a loud, sudden clanking. Now the clanking stops. All you hear is a man's low, threatening growl.

You start to follow that.

It's very close. You're plunging after it, shoving cornstalks aside. Now, without warning, you lurch right into a huddle of people, knocking hard into the hunched-over man. You both fall, flailing, over the figures crouched at the man's feet.

Turn to page 102.

The judge steps back from the antislavery men. He draws a folded sheet of paper from his coat pocket.

"Let me recite a moment," he says, unfolding the page. The big men blink in surprise. The judge begins.

"All men are born equally free and independent and have certain natural, inherent, and inalienable rights," he orates. *"Therefore no male person born in this country, or brought from over sea, ought to be holden by law to serve any person as a servant, slave or apprentice.*

"Do any of you know those words?" the judge asks.

Go on to the next page.

"Sure," says a shopkeeper. "That's the U.S. Constitution."

"No, my friend, it isn't," the judge says. "That is the *Vermont* Constitution—the first one in the United States to outlaw slavery. I intend to uphold our constitution today, as it is my sworn duty to do. If you men will let me pass, you will not be ashamed at the result."

The antislavers look at Henry Briggam, their leader.

He studies the judge. Then he nods.

The men step aside.

You gaze over at your father. He thinks abolitionists are high and mighty—but he believes in the law. Still, you have to wonder: if this country is filled with men who are this angry about slavery on one side and about property rights on the other, how long will words on paper hold them apart?

As you're wondering, the man in the pale suit rushes up. He's waving a paper of his own.

Turn to page 110.

They're hiding the captured slaves by the *railroad tracks*.

This can only mean one thing. The Vermont Central passenger train comes to town at eight o'clock every evening, on its way south to White River Junction. That's the reason they'd bring captives to Slab City—to slip them onto the train!

Everyone around here has heard of the capture, and many people are outraged. On the train the slave hunters and their captives will quickly get out of town. Then, at White River Junction, just an hour away, they'll pick up the express to New York and be gone.

Carstairs strides past the town's little train station. Along the tracks above it is a long, open shed for lumber being loaded on the freight trains. A few small houses stand beyond. He goes into one of those.

Turn to page 22.

You leap off the porch and tear up the street. But when you get to the corner, you turn back. Suddenly the whole second floor of the little wood home explodes in flames.

You sag against a maple tree. Flickering orange firelight shines through the tears that fill your eyes. In years to come, as a Union volunteer in the Civil War, you will see young men die by the hundreds—by the thousands. But this sight right now, of an old Northern house going up like a torch, is one awful vision that will haunt you the rest of your life.

The End

"As thee heard," Zeb whispers, "the cargo will arrive after dark. If we don't get it off tonight, with time to reach Montpelier before daylight, we run a great risk of discovery. The slave hunters are in town close by."

"Zeb, I want to help," you say. "Maybe I should. But there's something I must tell you. I've found out where the other ones are being held. The ones they've captured. They're here in town, and if I don't do something before the next train, they'll be riding back to slavery."

Zeb blinks at you.

"I did not know of this," he whispers.

"I kind of wish I didn't, either," you say. "But I do. What should I do?"

"It's a very difficult choice," the young Quaker says. "Perhaps the captives can be freed, some-how—but I cannot help thee do that."

"I know you can't."

"Perhaps the one who isn't yet captive has a better chance of reaching freedom," Zeb says. "But only with help."

"Can you find a conductor without me?"

"I can surely try," Zeb says. "But thee knows this village so well . . . thee must seek thy own light on this choice. I know thee will find it."

Go on to the next page.

Your friend grips your shoulder.

"If thee doesn't come back here, I'll know thee has chosen to help the captives," he says.

You step out into the evening. It's getting dark. There doesn't seem to be much light around anywhere, just now. How can you choose?

If you try to help the captives on your own, turn to page 81.

If you become part of the new Underground Railroad station, turn to page 26.

Quick as a cat the slave hunter has you on your back. His knee presses your chest. In one hand he still holds the heavy chain to which his captives are connected. With his other hand he's reaching inside his shirt.

"You shouldn't've meddled in other people's business," the man hisses at you. His eyes are gleaming. "Now no one's gonna find you for a *long* time."

From his shirt he pulls out a tiny derringer pistol. The gun is small but the barrel large enough as he holds it up. From that barrel comes a flash.

Early the next morning a passing townsman notices something dark and hunched over across the railroad tracks near the cornfield. He investigates to find the body of Dickey, who passed out from loss of blood and died quietly in the night.

Turn to page 61.

You turn to see the scruffy-looking slave hunter step out from behind a nearby tree. His pistol is large and near, and he has just drawn the hammer back.

"Here's as far north as you go, girl," he says. She lunges away—but he darts ahead and grabs her arm. He twists the arm behind her and puts the gun to her temple.

"Got her!" the man calls down to Shelby Winton. "Be right down." He turns to you. "Don't try nothin'. Ain't no use now."

"How'd you find us?" you ask.

"Why, I doubled back on foot," he says, pulling out a thick cord and winding it around the girl's wrists. "Saw everythin', includin' that business with the hay. Sneakin' up on you two was nothin'. We're hunters, you know. Good ones."

You watch, feeling sunk in helplessness, as the man binds the girl's wrists behind her back. Now he lifts the rope roughly upward. The girl's breath catches in pain as she is forced to her feet. He turns back to you.

"Don't you mess with runaways again, kid," he says.

But you can only stare. The two dark shapes work their way down the slope, the man roughly prodding the bent-over girl.

She wanted to *know* about things. She had a spark. Now you know what a slave is like. At least you know what this one was like.

She was like you.

The End

Crossing the bridge again, you slip into the tavern stable. The warm air smells of leather, hay, and horses. Dickey the stable boy is brushing down one of four horses.

"'Course I heard about it," he says. "These are the slave hunters' horses. They came in before dawn. They took a big load inside, all wrapped up in a buffalo robe—and squirming." He scowls and brushes hard.

"They brought 'em down to Slab City? Why?" you ask. "Why didn't they take 'em back along the stage road, the way they came?"

"That's the big secret, *I* think," Dickey says. "A little while after they came, they sneaked that same big load in here. They piled it into that livery." He points to the covered two-wheel coach in the corner. "Drove out fast. Still wasn't light yet. Nobody saw 'em. 'Cept me."

"Where'd they go?"

"Over the bridge. The livery was back pretty quick. They must've hid 'em somewhere in the village."

"Why? Why hide them at all?"

Dickey's eyes blaze. "You think folks around here are gonna sit by while slave hunters haul people in chains back south? These people are scum, and anyone helps 'em is dirt. They've got to smuggle those folks out of Slab City."

"How'll they do it?"

"Don't know," Dickey says. "But those slaves are hidden here in Slab City, somewhere, right now. Why don't you find out where?"

Turn to page 14.

You peer in the window of the train station. Sure enough, there in the flickering lamplight stand the slave hunter and his captives, the beautiful young black woman and her little boy. The white man grips the chain that is manacled to the other two. Bill Dobbs seems unconcerned. He's sitting at his desk behind the ticket window, nodding over some papers.

In the distance you hear a train's long whistle. Inside, as you watch, Dobbs stands up and speaks to the white man. He nods and begins to tug at the chain. Their faces set and without speaking, his two captives follow him toward the door to the platform.

You scamper around the side of the station. You can hear the heavy chugging of the train as it approaches. There, standing on the platform, are the men you've just routed from their homes.

Bill Dobbs's white-sleeved arm opens the station door and holds it for the slave hunter. Tugging the chain, he steps out, sees the men, and stops.

Turn to page 46.

The woman's slender wrist is clamped in a thick, black iron manacle. She lifts the arm higher: a heavy chain clanks a little. It connects her manacle to one on her son's arm.

Your eyes follow the chain on down. A third manacle lies unclasped on the floor. From it the chain is clamped onto the iron bedstead. A heavy padlock makes escape seem impossible.

"That empty iron—that *was* for my girl," the woman says. "But she slipped 'em. She's goin' to make it—she's bound to make it."

"Who is?"

"My girl. She's bound to reach the freedom land."

"What's that?" you ask. "Isn't *this* the freedom land?" That's what you learned in school— that this is the country of liberty.

But the woman just blinks at you.

"I . . . guess you mean Canada," you whisper. "If I can figure this out, maybe you can still get there."

The woman shakes her head. "I'm goin' to take care of us my own self."

Her strong eyes are locked on yours.

"If you want to help," she says, "you go get me a knife."

Turn to page 70.

That's how you come to be perched beside Nat Woodard the hill farmer as his two skinny horses draw the rough farm wagon up the long hill toward the ridgetop village called the Center.

Behind the plank that you two are sitting on is a pile of cut hay. Every now and then from within the pile comes a stifled sneeze.

"Yep," Nat says, answering a question you've just asked. "They did arrest 'im."

"They arrested Mister *Griswold*? Will he go to jail?"

"If he does, maybe I'll bust 'im out myself," says the farmer. He smiles thinly, which might mean that's a joke. Or maybe not.

"I don't understand why he does it," you say. "I mean, he's rich, and he's famous—at least around here. Why should a man like that risk going to prison to help people who've got nothing—and who never stop coming, no matter how many you help?"

For a long time, Nat doesn't answer. Finally, flicking the reins, he says, "Did ye never hear the story of Margery Griswold?"

Turn to page 35.

110

"I hold here a bill of ownership for the slaves in this building," the Southerner announces.

"We'll stuff it down your throat," Henry Briggam growls.

"You will not," answers Zachariah Gray.

The men pause. The judge studies the slave hunter's paper. He hands it back.

"Sir," he says, "this state's constitution prohibits slavery. Slave ownership is illegal within the borders of Vermont. Therefore this paper of yours is not only invalid, it's illegal."

Carefully he tears the paper up and lets the pieces fall.

Now your father steps forward to face the slave hunter. "Some of us are not admirers of the abolitionists," he says. "We believe you Southerners have a right to your own business, without high-and-mighty Northerners telling you how to do it.

"But our law says all people in Vermont are free," he goes on. "I believe our people shouldn't be stealing slaves on *your* soil—but you won't be chaining up anybody on ours."

"What you're doing is wrong," the Southerner says. "The Fugitive Slave Act makes it unlawful to assist runaways."

"Our legislature has declared that law null and void in Vermont. It's a state matter," the judge says. "You're beaten, sir."

The Southerner turns angrily to the Vermont men.

"All right, you've won this battle," he shouts. "But we shall see who wins the war!"

Turn to page 28.

Downstairs in the print shop of the *Voice of Freedom*, there's a small closet where runaways wait for the next conductor. Jubilee pokes her head inside.

"It's clean, dry, and safe," Poland says. Jubilee nods. She steps into the darkness but turns around.

Her eyes are shining.

"Never used to think there was any really *good* white folks," she says to you and Mrs. Flint. "Now I've known so many, and I never knew any of their names. But I know your names. And I won't ever forget 'em."

Grace Flint smiles. "We'll never forget yours, either," she says. "How could anyone forget a name like Jubilee?"

"It means somethin', you know," the girl says. She turns to you. "You know what it means."

"I do," you answer. "And that day's coming, Jubilee. When it comes, you and I will visit. We'll take a walk—right out in the open."

Jubilee nods. "By the way," she says, unbuttoning Nat Woodard's shirt, "tell that old farmer thank-you for me." She hands the shirt to you and steps back into the darkness.

Mister Poland closes the door.

Turn to page 117.

As soon as they're gone, Nat stops the wagon.

"I expect he's right," he says to you. "We won't get far before they're back with the sheriff."

"What should we do?"

The hill farmer stares ahead.

"I kin see two choices," he says. "One is you take our passenger off the road and hide for a spell. I'll keep goin'. By the time they catch up with me, they'll have no idea where you went."

"But then what?"

"Well, then we'd finish our journey. This way would prob'ly be the surest choice—except that you two'd be out here in the night on your own."

"What's the other choice?"

Nat eyes you. "Kin you ride?"

"Yes."

"I kin unhook one of the horses. I've got a riding bridle in the wagon. You two could hightail it for Montpelier. I'll slow 'em down long as I can. Trouble is, you still might not outrun 'em.

"It ain't easy," Nat allows. "But you'd best make the choice."

If you leave the wagon and hide in the night, turn to page 39.

If you try to outride the slave hunters, turn to page 10.

After sleeping until almost noon, you and Jubilee have had two full meals—first a pile of hotcakes, bacon, and syrup, then a supper of ham, eggs, and biscuits, not to mention two large batches of steaming doughnuts in between. Jubilee has told you about all the places she's been hidden—in barrels and haylofts, in secret rooms behind chimneys, in dank cellars and cobwebbed barns. She's told of all the ways she and her family traveled: always at night, first on foot through swamps and across fields, then hidden in wagons and carriages and on horseback along every kind of road, from Maryland up through Delaware, across the Delaware River on a midnight boat, through the marshes, pines, and hills of New Jersey, then night after night through New England. All the while they never knew where they were, who was helping them, or when they might be caught.

"I never ever slept in a bed before last night, ma'am," she says as you start up the road. "Not ever."

"Well, child, you'll sleep in many more of 'em," Grace Flint answers. "After we get to Montpelier tonight, you're just a couple of nights away from Canada."

Turn to page 66.

114

The bed comes apart—but the heavy chain that's manacled to the woman and her little boy does not. Somehow you're going to have to get the two of them out the window, across the little porch, and down to the ground without any noise that the guard downstairs can hear.

Can you do it? You've got to try.

Holding your forefinger to your lips to urge the little boy to be silent, you pick up the heavy chain and the empty manacle meant for the woman's daughter. The woman picks up the chain at the other end. It clinks, but not loudly, as you all inch in an awkward clump toward the window.

The woman swings one leg out the window. Sitting on the sill, she reaches down to lift her boy. He's calm at first—but once she starts to swing him out onto the sloping roof, he panics and starts kicking and flailing.

Struggling to hold him, the woman loses her balance and tips backward. Her eyes surge in panic as she grabs at the windowframe. You lunge to grab her, dropping the empty manacle.

The heavy iron wrist cuff bangs on the floor. You catch the woman and steady her. Quickly, because of the noise, she drops her son on the roof—too heavily.

You hear heavy footsteps on the stairs.

Turn to page 68.

As quietly as you can, not to rouse your dad, you open the back door and step into the kitchen.

Your mother starts to say something, but you hold your hand to your lips. You motion her to follow you outside.

"Pa can't hear this," you whisper.

She nods again.

"Ma, I found 'em. The fugitives—the ones they caught."

"You *found* them?"

"Yes. Ma, you were right—it's a lady and a little boy. Why do you figure the slave catchers want 'em so bad?"

"There's got to be a big reward for them," your mother says. "That's always what the slave catchers are after. Judging by that handbill I had to typeset for the girl, the rewards for this woman and her children must be very large."

"But why?"

She shakes her head. "I don't know."

You think of how little time you've got.

"Ma, I need a knife. That little sharp one you've got. Please let me borrow it—just for a little while."

Your mother draws in a sharp breath.

"A *knife*," she whispers. "Why, you're just a child. And those slave hunters—they've no care for human life. No. I'm sorry. No."

Now, for the sake of two lives, it's time to stretch the truth a little.

Turn to page 65.

Out on State Street, it's morning. You blink and yawn. Your body is heavy as lead—and you've got a whole day's ride home ahead of you.

"This work ain't easy, is it, Mrs. Flint? Night after night we'll be going with no sleep at all."

"That's true," says your new fellow conductor as you help her into the carriage. "But when some trains come along, you've just got to ride them."

The End

C
G   h
te
with
v ntur
Wing
nia.